Josie Smith

at Christmas

Collins

Also by Magdalen Nabb

Josie Smith
Josie Smith at School
Josie Smith at the Seaside
Josie Smith and Eileen
Josie Smith in Hospital
Josie Smith at the Market
The Enchanted Horse

MAGDALEN NABB

Josie Smith

at Christmas

Illustrated by Pirkko Vainio

CollinsChildren'sBooks
An Imprint of HarperCollinsPublishers

First published by Collins Children's Books 1992
This edition published 1995

3 5 7 9 8 6 4

CollinsChildren'sBooks is a division of
HarperCollins*Publishers* Ltd,
77-85 Fulham Palace Road,
Hammersmith, London W6 8JB

Text copyright © Magdalen Nabb 1992
Illustrations copyright © Pirkko Vainio 1992

The author and illustrator assert the moral right to be
identified as the author and illustrator of the work.

Printed and bound in Great Britain by
Caledonian International Book Manufacturing Ltd, Glasgow

ISBN 0 00 674537 7

Contents

Contents

Josie Smith and the Angel

It was a dark and snowy afternoon. The lights were on in Josie Smith's classroom and all the children were making a lot of noise. The floor was wet from everybody's wellingtons, there was a smell of school dinner, and wet gloves were drying on the radiators because they'd all been snowballing and sliding and falling in the yard.

"Quiet, everybody," Miss Valentine said. But they were all shouting and pushing and nobody could hear.

"If you've all got your gym shoes on," Miss Valentine said, "start moving your tables and chairs. And do it quietly!"

They started moving their tables and chairs but they didn't do it quietly. They pushed and shoved and crashed and banged and shouted and argued and scraped and bumped, and then the door opened and Miss Potts, the headmistress, marched in.

"How dare you!" shouted Miss Potts, "How dare you make all this noise that I can hear from my office!"

Everybody stopped. It went so quiet that you could hear the children breathing, and Josie Smith could hear her own chest going bam bam bam because she was frightened of Miss Potts.

"What's going on in here?" roared Miss Potts.

"They're just moving their tables and chairs," Miss Valentine said, "so they can practise their Nativity play."

"Moving their tables and chairs!" roared Miss Potts. "And is that how you carry a chair? Rawley Baxter! I'm talking to you!" And she marched up to Rawley Baxter and roared down at him.

"You pick a chair up by its seat, you don't drag it about by its back! If I hear about any broken chairs in this classroom I'll have your parents in! Is that understood?" Everybody

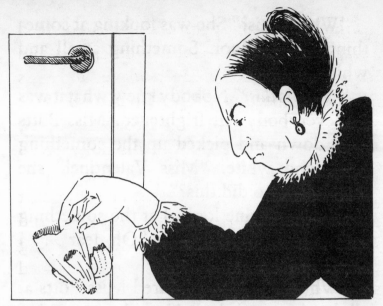

said, "Yes, Miss Potts." And then Eileen said in a soppy voice, "Miss Potts, I'm carrying my chair the right way."

"I should think so, too!" roared Miss Potts. "And another thing! I've had one boy in my office this afternoon for throwing snowballs with stones in them. Now, if I hear of one more child throwing snowballs with stones in them there'll be no more snowballing in my yard. Is that understood? Thank you, Miss Valentine."

Miss Potts went stamping towards the door. But just as she was going to open it, she stopped.

"What's this?" She was looking at something on the floor. Something small and white.

"What is *this*?" Nobody knew what it was but everybody felt frightened. Miss Potts bent down and picked up the something small and white. "Miss Valentine!" she roared, "Who did this?"

Miss Valentine looked at the something small and white and said, "Oh dear . . . I don't know."

"Who broke this?" roared Miss Potts at all the class, and she held up the something small and white for everyone to see.

It was the angel from the Christmas crib on the cupboard.

The shiny white pottery angel with pointy hands and golden wings and long curly hair.

"Just look at it!" roared Miss Potts.

Everybody looked.

The shiny white angel had no head and no pointy hands and the tips of its golden wings were gone.

Nobody said anything.

Then Eileen said in a soppy voice, "Miss

Potts, Gary Grimes broke it. Miss Potts, he was messing with it and I saw him."

Eileen was always telling over people.

"I never!" Gary Grimes said, and he looked really scared.

"I'll have your parents in about this, Gary Grimes! And don't think this class is getting another angel out of my cupboard for that crib. You'll do without! Now get on quietly! Thank you, Miss Valentine." And she marched out, banging the door.

They finished moving their tables and chairs and then they all stood in the middle of the classroom and waited. They weren't making a noise any more and everybody felt fed up. Gary Grimes came near Eileen and put his fist up near her face.

"I'll get you for that," he whispered, "Tell-tale-tit!"

"A-aw!" Eileen said, "I'm telling over you for calling me names."

Josie Smith said, "You shouldn't keep telling over people." Eileen was Josie Smith's best friend but she was horrible sometimes.

"Settle down," Miss Valentine said, and they started practising their Nativity play.

They stood in their places and Rawley Baxter shouted, "Behold!" Then he stopped. He was being one of the three kings but he didn't like it. He only liked being Batman.

"Behold!" he shouted again, but he couldn't remember what came next. The second king nudged him to make him carry on but Rawley Baxter turned round and thumped him and said, "Don't shove!"

"Rawley!" said Miss Valentine, "We have followed a bright star."

"Miss Valentine, he always forgets,"

Eileen said. She was being an angel and she was going to have wings like the one on the crib only now it was broken.

"Start again," Miss Valentine said. "And Gary Grimes, sit still. If you break anything else today, you'll really be in trouble."

Gary Grimes was sitting in a chair by himself. He wasn't being in the Nativity play because he was going in hospital soon to have his tonsils out. Josie Smith and Ann Lomax and Christine Tattersall might be having their tonsils out, too, but they hadn't had a letter yet to say when they had to go in hospital. Miss Valentine let them be in the play but they didn't have to say anything and they didn't have costumes, just in case they wouldn't be there. They just had to sit cross-legged on the floor and be called Children Bearing Gifts. Josie Smith thought about Eileen wearing a long white frock and wings and she wanted to cry but she didn't.

"Rawley," said Miss Valentine, "please try to remember it by yourself just once. You haven't got so much to say, now have you?"

"No," said Rawley Baxter, pulling a

13

horrible face and fiddling with the plastic Batman in his pocket.

"Well start again, then. And this time get it right."

Rawley Baxter thought for a bit and then he shouted, "Behold!" And then he stopped. He thought for a long time and everybody waited to see if he'd remember.

"Don't tell him, anybody," Miss Valentine said. Rawley Baxter was still thinking. Then he shouted, "Behold! I bring you tidings of great joy!"

"You don't say that!" Miss Valentine said, "It's the first angel who says that to the shepherds. Oh, for goodness' sake!"

Then the bell rang for home time.

Josie Smith and Eileen put their coats on and Josie Smith put her itchy scarf on, winding it round and round so she wouldn't get tonsillitis. Then she put her hood up. Eileen had a pink knitted hat with strings and pompoms. Miss Valentine had to tie it for her. Eileen lifted her chin up so Miss Valentine could tie a bow and said, "Miss Valentine, Gary Grimes is always breaking things. He's naughty."

"It was an accident," Miss Valentine said. "He didn't mean to break it, but it is a shame. The crib's not so nice without an angel. I wonder if we could make one."

"I can make one," Josie Smith said. "My mum'll help me."

"I can make one," Eileen said. "My mum will help me."

"I can make one," shouted somebody else.

"I can make one," shouted everybody.

"You can all try and make one," Miss Valentine said. "And the best one can go on the crib. Now all of you go straight home because it's getting very dark."

Some people remembered their gloves on the radiator and some people didn't. Eileen put on her pink knitted mittens that were sewn inside her coat sleeves on strings. She never had to put her gloves on the radiator because she never played snowballs.

When they were ready they stood in a line and said, "Goo-daf-ter-noon-Miss-Val-en-tine."

Then they set off home.

It was freezing cold and dark and the

snow, that had been soft enough for
snowballs when the sun was out, was
getting crisp and icy. There were brown
lines in the lamplit road where some cars
had gone past. Josie Smith didn't like the
snow so much when it got dirty.

"I wish it would snow again," she said.

"I don't," Eileen said, "because you have
to wear wellingtons and your socks go down
inside them and hurt."

Josie Smith always wore her wellingtons
because she liked them. She could climb
and kick and splash in them without getting
shouted at.

16

When they got to Mr Scowcroft's allotment Eileen said, "I bet you're not really going to make an angel for the crib."

"Oh yes I am," said Josie Smith, "with golden hair and wings."

"I am as well, then," Eileen said.

But Josie Smith was best at making things so she didn't care. She stamped along in her wellingtons and kicked at the snow to make it fly about.

"Stop kicking," Eileen said, "It's all going down our wellingtons." Then something hit her on her woolly hat and she shouted, "Ow!"

A lot of boys ran off in the dark down one of the backs and Josie Smith heard Rawley Baxter singing, "Da-da-da-da-da-da-da-da Da-da-da-da-da-da-da-da Batman!"

Eileen started to run home crying.

"Meh–her–her–her!" she roared. "I'm telling my mum! There was a stone in that snowball and I'm telling! Meh–her–her–her!"

Josie Smith ran after her, her wellingtons sliding in the snow. She was frightened of falling but she had to catch up with Eileen.

"Wait!" she shouted. "Wait for me! There wasn't a stone in it. It was just an ordinary snowball! Rawley Baxter threw it and he never puts stones in snowballs! Wait!"

But Eileen was turning the corner, still crying, and Josie Smith saw her woolly hat bobbing in the light under the lamp post.

"Wait for me! Eileen!"

Josie Smith skidded round the corner and caught hold of the cold iron lamp post so she wouldn't fall. But Eileen ran in at her own front door, crying a lot louder now that she knew her mum could hear her.

Josie Smith stopped running. She could

see her breath like smoke in the yellow lamplight and her chest was going bam bam bam. She stamped the snow off her wellingtons on the doorstep and went in.

"Mum!" she shouted, "Eileen's going to tell over Rawley Baxter for throwing snowballs with stones in them and he didn't because it was only an ordinary snowball, I saw it, and Mum, if she tells, Miss Potts won't let us play snowballs any more!"

"Take your wellingtons off," said Josie's mum, "before you come in here. I have to tell you every day." Josie's mum was sewing the hem of a skirt she was making for Eileen's mum. "And put your slippers on," she said.

Josie Smith took her wellingtons off and left them on the mat near the door. When she walked to the kitchen in stockinged feet it hurt because her socks had rolled right down under her heels. When she pulled them up they were a bit wet and some pieces of ice were stuck to them.

"My feet are freezing," said Josie Smith. "And my hands as well."

"Take those wet socks off and put your

19

slippers on, I've just told you," said Josie's
mum, holding the skirt up and shaking it.
"And don't stand near the fire, you'll get
chilblains."

Josie Smith took her socks off and then
her coat.

"Where are your gloves?" said Josie's
mum.

Josie Smith felt in her coat pockets but she
couldn't find them.

"If you've lost those gloves you'll get no
more," said Josie's mum. "See that you find

them and then I'll sew them into your sleeves like Eileen."

"But, Mum!" said Josie Smith, "if you have them sewn into your sleeves you can't play snowballs because you can't put them to dry on the radiator."

Then she remembered. "I haven't lost them. I left them on the radiator at school."

"Set the table," said Josie's mum. And she went and put the kettle on and started cutting bread with a bad-tempered look on her face.

Josie Smith wanted to ask if she could make an angel after tea but when she looked at the creases in her mum's forehead she didn't say anything. She set the table and her mum made some bacon and eggs and chips and fried tomatoes. Then she drew the curtains across the steamy window and they sat down at the table.

Josie Smith was hungry and thirsty and she ate everything on her plate and two pieces of bread and butter and a big cup of sweet tea. But her mum wasn't hungry. She poured herself a cup of tea and put her hand over her eyes and said, "Oh, I've got such a splitting headache. I wonder if I need glasses."

"Can I have glasses, as well?" asked Josie Smith.

"There's nothing wrong with your eyes," said Josie's mum.

"Julie Horrocks in my class has got glasses," said Josie Smith.

"She's got a lazy eye," said Josie's mum.

"What's a lazy eye?" asked Josie Smith.

"Don't pester," said Josie's mum. "Finish your tea. I'm going to put my feet up and I want five minutes' peace."

So Josie's mum sat in the chair by the kitchen fire and put her feet up and Josie Smith waited.

She sat on the rug and didn't make a noise. After a bit her toes warmed up and started tickling. She took her itchy slippers off and felt them. Her toes were very red and although they felt cold when she touched them with her warm hands they were burning inside and getting itchier and itchier. She knew she shouldn't rub them. "I'll not put my slippers back on, though," she said to herself, "because they're

scratchy." She wished she had some fur-lined slippers with pompoms on like Eileen's. She wished she could have some for Christmas. She rubbed her red toes against the rug just a little bit and thought about Christmas while she waited for five minutes to go past.

She thought about Christmas cards with robins on them like her gran always sent and Christmas pudding and a mince pie to leave on the fender for Father Christmas and crayoning holly with dark green pointy leaves and red berries and the cotton wool snow on Mrs Chadwick's shop window and Christmas decorations and muffins and jelly at the school party. Then she looked at the clock on the mantelpiece and said, "Mum?"

But her mum's eyes were closed and she still had creases in her forehead. Josie Smith's red toes burned hotter and hotter. She rubbed them just a little bit more on the rug and thought about slippers with pompoms on and a shiny new book wrapped in Christmas paper and a bag of new marbles and red and green crepe paper round the light shades in the classroom and sticky dates in a box with a frill round and camels on the lid and camels with kings bearing gifts and the ox and the ass in the straw and the broken angel. Then she looked at the clock on the mantelpiece and said, "Mum?"

But her mum's eyes were closed and she still had creases in her forehead. A lot more than five minutes had gone past. If Josie's mum woke up now she'd say "Get ready for bed."

Josie Smith got up from the rug very

quietly and got her tin of cutting-out things. Then she sat down again and looked at what was inside. There was some cardboard saved from cereal boxes and some silver and gold paper saved from chocolate bars. There was a bit of glue and a lace paper doily from her gran's and a tiny bit of glitter in a tube that Eileen had given her. There were two sheets of clean white writing paper that her mum had given her to make her Christmas cards: one for her gran and one for Aunty Helen who lived in London. She was going to fold

them in four and crayon holly and robins on them.

Josie Smith pulled out the sheets of clean paper and sat thinking about them. If she used them to make the angel, perhaps her mum wouldn't give her any more to make Christmas cards. But you can't make an angel out of dirty old cardboard from a cereal box. Angels are clean and white. Josie Smith got her scissors out and started work.

She made a big cone of white paper for the angel's frock and put a white frill round it made of lace paper doily. Then she made a small cone for its head. She cut a long strip of paper with a pointy hand on each end and wrapped it round and stuck it at the back. Then she cut tiny strips of paper and curled them with her scissors to make angel hair. Then she cut out cardboard wings and smoothed gold paper on her knee to cover them. Last of all she sprinkled her precious bit of golden glitter over a stripe of glue round the bottom of the angel's frock.

There was no glitter left now for her Christmas cards but Josie Smith didn't care

because an angel had to be perfect or it wasn't an angel at all.

And it was perfect. Josie Smith knelt up and looked. The clean white angel was as pure and glistening as Christmas snow and it sparkled in the firelight like magic. Josie Smith held her breath and then she said, "Mum?"

"Mm?" said Josie's mum, and then with her eyes shut she said, "Get ready for bed."

"But, Mum," said Josie Smith, "I've made an angel. Look!"

Josie's mum opened her eyes a bit and said, "That's nice." She said it the way grown-ups do when they're not really looking, just to make you shut up. Then she opened her eyes properly and said, "That *is* nice!" Because she meant it. Then she said, "Are you going to put it on the Christmas tree?"

"No," said Josie Smith. "It's for school because Gary Grimes broke the angel off the crib."

Josie's mum sat up and said, "I'll find you a bag for it, then you can carry it to school without getting it dirty. Now get ready for bed."

All night the angel stood on the chest of drawers in Josie Smith's bedroom in its glittering white frock, and next morning it was snowing again.

"Mum!" shouted Josie Smith, when she opened her bedroom curtains, "It's snowing again!"

Big snowflakes were falling slowly into the yard and the black crowns of all the chimneys poked out of thick white fluffy blankets.

Josie Smith got dressed in her kilt and

29

blouse and cardigan as fast as she could and ran downstairs with her buttons done up all wrong.

"Can I go out in the yard?" she said.

"Eat your breakfast," said Josie's mum, "or you'll be late for school."

"But then can I?" asked Josie Smith.

"If there's time," said Josie's mum.

Josie Smith ate her breakfast as fast as she could and then she put her coat and wellingtons on and her itchy scarf and went out in the yard.

The snow in the yard was thick and soft and the knobbly black stones of the walls had little slices of snow in all their cracks. Josie Smith poked her finger into the clean snow and tasted some. Then she made some footprints right across the middle and walked back in them and made them go back to front. Then she stood still with her face to the sky. The snowflakes were twirling round and round and round and round right up as far as the top of the sky and they made Josie Smith feel dizzy. She shut her eyes and let the big snowflakes land on her face and tickle and burn and melt. It

was very quiet. She pulled her tongue out and a snowflake melted there.

Then her mum shouted, "Josie! Eileen's here!"

She gave Josie Smith the plastic bag with her angel in it and said, "Now there's a letter in there as well that you've to give to Miss Valentine. See that you don't forget."

And Josie Smith and Eileen set off in the snow to school.

"I've got tights on," Eileen said, "because they don't go down inside your wellingtons. And I've got a new cardigan on as well and it's pink with see-through buttons."

"I've made an angel," Josie Smith said.

Then Rawley Baxter ran past them with a lot of other boys and they were shouting and pushing each other in the snow.

Eileen shouted, "I'm telling over you, Rawley Baxter, for throwing snowballs with stones in them!"

But the boys took no notice. They were skidding and sliding about and throwing big handfuls of the soft snow at each other without bothering to make it into snowballs.

"Don't tell over him," Josie Smith said, "or we won't be able to play snowballs any more."

"I don't care," said Eileen. The snow-flakes were sticking to her pink knitted hat and now it was pink and white. "And anyway," she said, "I've brought an angel for the crib as well. I'll show it to you, if you want, when Rawley Baxter's gone in the yard. My mum said not to get it out when there were boys because they'll break it."

So they waited at the corner near Mr Scowcroft's allotment until all the boys had gone in through the gate and were playing in the school yard. Josie Smith poked her bare finger in the snow on Mr Scowcroft's fence and looked at the snowy cabbages growing on the other side. Eileen opened her pink satchel.

"You'll have to help me," Eileen said, "because I have to open the box and undo the tissue paper without ripping anything or spoiling the Sellotape. I'm not really supposed to open it before I get to school." Josie Smith hung her plastic bag carefully on the snowy fence and helped Eileen to

unstick the Sellotape and open the parcel
without spoiling it.

Then she looked at Eileen's angel.

"Do you like it?" Eileen said.

But Josie Smith just stared.

Eileen's angel lay in its tissue paper and
its dress was glistening white velvet and its
yellow hair was long and wavy just like real
hair. Its wings were made of tiny velvety
feathers and it carried a little golden trumpet
in its hands. It was the purest white and
prettiest thing that Josie Smith had ever seen.

She thought about her poor paper angel and held her breath so she wouldn't cry.

"How did you make it?" said Josie Smith, and her chest was going bam bam bam because she'd always been the best at making things and she couldn't make anything as good as that.

"It's a secret," Eileen said. And then she said, "I'll tell you, if you want, because you're my best friend, only you have to promise not to tell over me."

"I never tell over people," said Josie Smith.

"Cross your heart and hope to die?"

"All right. Cross my heart and hope to die."

Eileen put her pink woolly hat covered in cold snowflakes near to Josie Smith's ear. Then she looked to see if anybody was near and then she put her hand to her mouth and whispered,

"My mum bought it from Mr Bowker's, the newsagent's. She took me after school yesterday because I was crying. It cost heaps of money."

Josie Smith pushed away from Eileen. Her

face felt hot and red. "You weren't supposed to buy it!" she said. "You were supposed to make it. Miss Valentine said!"

"I know she did but I don't care," Eileen said, "because nobody knows and you can't tell because you said 'Cross my heart and hope to die.'"

"It's not fair!" shouted Josie Smith.

"Oh yes it is," said Eileen, "because I got hit with a snowball *and* there was a stone in it, so my mum said I could buy something nice because I was upset."

"Oh no it is *not* fair," Josie Smith said. "And you're soft and if you tell over Rawley Baxter I'm not being your best friend!"

"I don't care," said Eileen. "I'll tell over him if I want. I'm going in now to give my angel to Miss Valentine." And she went off with her pink satchel and her pink woolly hat with snowflakes stuck to it and Josie Smith shouted after her, "I'm not coming to school with you and I'm not playing with you at playtime and I'm not helping you with your drawing if we have drawing so don't bother asking me! And I don't like your horrible angel, anyway!" But she said that bit with her eyes shut because it was a lie.

Eileen went in at the school gate and Josie Smith stood by Mr Scowcroft's fence in the snow and watched. Everyone was running and shouting and laughing in the yard and the snow was falling faster and faster but Josie Smith didn't like it so much any more.

She stood near the fence by herself and the snowflakes stuck to her hair and her coat and floated down inside her wellingtons and she thought about Eileen's shiny velvet angel and cried. Then she thought about her poor paper angel and hated it, and then she cried because she felt sorry for hating it. It wasn't the angel's fault that Eileen was horrible.

The snowflakes melted on her bare hands and she put them in her pockets because they were freezing cold. Then she saw the children in the yard lining up and going in and she got frightened of being late. She wiped her eyes on her snowy sleeves and ran as fast as she could to school.

As soon as they were in their classroom Miss Valentine said, "Look everybody! Look what Eileen's brought for our crib!"

All the girls went Ooooooh! And even the boys liked it because of the tiny golden trumpet. Miss Valentine made Eileen stand at the front and they all had to clap her to say Thank you. Josie Smith clapped.

Rawley Baxter said, "She bought that from Mr Bowker's. We've got two on our Christmas tree." But he didn't tell Miss Valentine.

School was horrible all day. They had some hard sums to do and Josie Smith got them all wrong and it was a horrible dinner and nobody could play snowballing after because Eileen had told. They made a slide instead and Josie Smith fell on it and hurt her knee but she only got ointment on it and no plaster. In the afternoon they had to practise their Nativity play and Josie Smith sat cross-legged on the floor with Ann Lomax and Christine Tattersall being Children Bearing Gifts and feeling tired and fed up.

When it was home time, Miss Valentine said, "Josie, don't forget your gloves today. They're still on the radiator." And when Josie Smith was putting them on, she said, "I thought you might have made me an angel, Josie."

Josie Smith tried to say that she had made one, but a lump came in her throat so she didn't say it properly and then Rawley Baxter started pushing in the line and Miss Valentine went to tell him off.

Outside it was dark and freezing and the slide in the yard shone like glass in the light from the windows. Gary Grimes ran at it and slid and sat down with a bump. Eileen laughed at him and he came up to her with his fist up and said, "You've had it, you have! Rawley Baxter's going to get you for telling over him!"

"I don't care!" shouted Eileen, but she was so scared she started running home. Josie Smith didn't run after her. At the gate Ann Lomax came up to Josie Smith and said, "If you're not being Eileen's best friend you can be mine. You can come to our house and I'll give you a bracelet."
Josie Smith didn't say anything. Ann Lomax had hundreds of bracelets but when she gave you one she always wanted it back after. It was never for keeps. Josie Smith walked home, stamping her wellingtons because her feet were freezing. When she got in she could smell something good frying for tea but when she went in the kitchen to see what it was, her mum said, "Did you give that note to Miss Valentine?"

Josie Smith stood still in the warm kitchen and her chest was going bam bam bam because she couldn't remember a note.

"Well?" said Josie's mum. "You didn't forget?"

Josie Smith was feeling in her coat pocket

but there was no note there. What note? She couldn't remember anything about a note.

"You forgot, didn't you?" said Josie's mum.

"I don't know," said Josie Smith. She closed her eyes a bit because she couldn't remember whether she'd forgotten or not.

"It was in the bag with your angel," said Josie's mum.

Josie Smith felt hot and frightened. She couldn't remember the note but she remembered the angel. Where was the bag with the angel?

"Well?" said Josie's mum. "Have you lost your tongue?"

"I've lost my angel," said Josie Smith, trying not to cry.

"You'd lose your head if it wasn't screwed on," said Josie's mum. "Oh, never mind, I'll go and see Miss Valentine myself tomorrow. I'll have to ask her about your costume, anyway."

"I'm not having a costume," said Josie Smith. "You don't have a costume when you're Children Bearing Gifts."

"No," said Josie's mum. "But you do if you're an angel. Tinsel halo and wings and all. Now set the table for tea."

"Am I being an angel?" said Josie Smith. "An angel like Eileen bringing tidings of great joy?"

"That's right," said Josie's mum. "And do you know what that means? Tidings of great joy."

"It means good news," said Josie Smith. "Miss Valentine said."

"Well, the good news is," said Josie's mum, "that you're not going in hospital until after Christmas. That's what the note to Miss Valentine said and if you hadn't gone and lost it you could have been bearing tidings of great joy instead of bearing gifts at school today. Do you want another sausage?"

While they were eating their tea Josie Smith told her mum about Eileen's angel.

"She showed it to me when we were going to school," she said. "We stopped at Mr Scowcroft's allotment and –"

"And what?" said Josie's mum.

"And I left that bag with my angel on Mr

Scowcroft's fence! And it's been snowing! And now it's cold and dark and my angel's outside by itself and if the snow got into the bag it'll be wet!"

"You are a comic," said Josie's mum. But after tea they put their coats on and Josie's mum stood at the corner while Josie Smith ran as fast as her wellington's would go up the road to Mr Scowcroft's allotment in the dark on the crunchy snow. Then she ran all the way back with her bag.

"There was snow on it!" she shouted, "but it hasn't gone inside!"

Josie Smith took her angel up to bed with her and put it back on her chest of drawers where she could see its white shape in the dark. And in the dark she sang to it, very quietly, a Christmas carol about angels. And after that she whispered, "You can stay here with me. You don't have to go to school where you'd be by yourself at night. And when we get our Christmas tree you can be on it, and when I'm in the Nativity play I'll have a dress like yours. My mum's making it. If you listen, you can hear her sewing machine." They listened to the sewing machine downstairs and then Josie Smith whispered, "Anyway, you're better than Eileen's angel because I made you myself so we're friends."

After she'd sung another carol, Josie Smith fell asleep.

Outside in the dark and the cold the snow was freezing on Josie Smith's windowsill, and inside, warm and sheltered, Josie Smith's friendly angel stood near her on the chest of drawers and waited with her for Christmas.

Josie Smith and
The Fancy Dress Party

"I've got a surprise for you," said Josie's mum.

"What is it? What is it?" shouted Josie Smith.

"Don't shout," said Josie's mum, "And take your wellingtons off when you come in from school. How many times do I have to tell you?"

Josie Smith took her wellingtons off and put her itchy old slippers on her cold feet and washed her hands and face.

Then she said, "Now will you tell me?"

"Set the table," said Josie's mum. And then she laughed and said, "As soon as we're sitting at the table I'll tell you."

When they were sitting at the table, Josie Smith said, "Have you finished my angel's costume for the Nativity play? Is that the surprise?"

"No, I haven't," said Josie's mum. "I won't be able to finish it before Sunday. I've a frock to make for Mrs Chadwick. The surprise is you're going to a fancy dress party."

"What's a fancy dress party?" asked Josie Smith. "Do you have to wear a fancy dress?"

"You have to wear a costume," said Josie's mum.

"A bathing costume?" said Josie Smith.

"No!" said Josie's mum. "A costume like your angel's costume. All the children who go have to dress up as something. A witch or a cowboy or a fairy or something like that."

"And what will I be dressed as?" asked Josie Smith.

"I don't know yet," said Josie's mum. "We'll have to see what we can find."

"And will Eileen be going as well?" asked Josie Smith, because Eileen was Josie Smith's best friend.

"Eileen'll be going as well," said Josie's mum. "It's Eileen's dad who'll be taking you

both because it's being run by the factory where he works."

"And what's Eileen going to be dressed as?" asked Josie Smith.

"I don't know," said Josie's mum. "You'll have to ask her."

The next day, when they were going to school in the snow, Josie Smith asked her.

"It's a secret," Eileen said. "But I'll tell you, if you want, because you're my best friend." And she stopped and whispered in Josie Smith's ear. "I'm going as Little

Bo Peep and I'm having a crinoline dress and a shepherd's crook and a woolly lamb to carry."

"A real lamb?" asked Josie Smith.

"No, a toy one," Eileen said. "But it's made of real sheepskin, my mum said."

All day at school Josie Smith thought about the crinoline dress and the shepherd's crook and the toy lamb made of real sheepskin. When it was playtime she still hadn't finished her sums and in the afternoon when they had drawing she tried to draw a lady in a crinoline dress but it came out horrible. And, worst of all, Eileen had her best new cardigan on, the pink one with see-through buttons. Josie Smith was fed up because her cardigan was fawn and itchy and it had brown buttons.

At home time it was dark and foggy and all the snow was dirty and melting. Josie Smith stamped the slush off her wellingtons at the front doorstep and went in. There was a fire in the front room and Josie's mum was sewing on her machine. She was sewing something dark blue with shiny satin and net and glittery ribbon.

"Is it for me?" shouted Josie Smith. "Is it my costume for the fancy dress party?" She didn't care about Eileen's woolly lamb if she could have a blue net frock with glittery ribbon.

"No, it's not," said Josie's mum. "This is for Mrs Chadwick."

Josie Smith stared at the blue satin and net and the glittery ribbon and tried to think of Mrs Chadwick in the shop across the road wearing it, but she couldn't.

"Are you pulling my leg?" asked Josie Smith. "And is it really my costume for the fancy dress party?"

But Josie's mum only said, "I haven't had a minute to think about your costume, but don't worry, we'll find something."

"I wish I could have a blue net frock," said Josie Smith.

"Set the table," said Josie's mum. "Your tea'll not be long."

"But the fancy dress party's tomorrow," said Josie Smith, and some tears came in her eyes and she thought about Eileen in her crinoline dress.

"Wash your hands," said Josie's mum.

"But why does Mrs Chadwick want a blue net frock with glittery ribbon?" asked Josie Smith when they were having their tea. "She always wears an overall."

"Because she's going to a dance," said Josie's mum. "On Christmas Eve."

"If there's a bit of net left," said Josie Smith, "can I have it for my costume?"

"We'll see," said Josie's mum.

"But it's *tomorrow*!" said Josie Smith.

"Don't pester," said Josie's mum. "Clear

the table. If I finish Mrs Chadwick's dance frock tonight, I'll see about your costume."

Josie Smith stayed up as late as she could to see if her mum would finish Mrs Chadwick's frock, but she didn't. Then she lay in bed with her eyes wide open and tried to stay awake until the sewing machine stopped, but she couldn't.

Then it was Saturday morning.

"Josie!" shouted Josie's mum. "Come down and get your breakfast!"

When Josie Smith went down she saw Mrs Chadwick's dance frock on a hanger on the door.

"Is it finished?" asked Josie Smith.

"Nearly," said Josie's mum. "I've just the hem to do when she's tried it on."

"And is there some net left for me?" asked Josie Smith.

"Only a tiny piece," said Josie's mum.

"Is it enough for a costume?" asked Josie Smith.

"It's just a scrap," said Josie's mum. "Now stop pestering about your costume, we'll find something. There's an old jumper of mine, now I think about it, that might be just the thing. If you've finished your breakfast, get your coat on and we'll go and do the shopping."

They put their coats and itchy scarves on and went out into the busy Saturday morning street. The snow was all gone. There were dirty brown footprints all over the pavement and dirty brown slush along the road and dirty brown fog above all the black chimneys. The lights were on in all the shops. Josie Smith wanted to cry. She didn't want to go shopping and she didn't want to wear a horrible old jumper to the fancy dress party.

They queued up in the butcher's where everybody was talking and it smelled of sawdust and wet coats and fat. Then they queued up in the greengrocer's where everybody was talking and it smelled of celery and big boiled beetroots. Then they queued up in Mrs Chadwick's where everybody was talking and it smelled of soap and cakes. Then they left their shopping bags just inside the front door and went up the road to the newsagent's.

Josie Smith liked it at the newsagent's.

She liked Mr Bowker behind the counter because he didn't talk so much and she liked the smell of newspapers and shiny magazines. Then there were exciting smells of new crayons and colouring books and pipe tobacco and Christmas decorations.

Josie's mum paid the newspaper bill and then she said, "Give me two sheets of coloured tissue paper."

Mr Bowker opened a long drawer and lifted out a beautiful pile of tissue paper in all the colours of the rainbow.

"What colour would you like?" he said.

But Josie's mum didn't choose.

"You choose," she said to Josie Smith. "The tissue paper's for you."

Josie Smith held her breath and tried and tried to choose. But there were four different pinks and four different blues and then all the reds and yellows and greens and purple and orange and black.

"Choose two different ones," said Josie's mum, "if you like."

After a long time, Josie Smith chose a deep blue like Mrs Chadwick's frock and a pink like Eileen's new cardigan. Mr Bowker folded them up without making creases and put them in a paper bag.

"Is it for my costume?" asked Josie Smith, as they went out, ringing the bell.

"For part of it," said Josie's mum. "You'll see."

Josie Smith got excited then. She splashed her wellingtons in the sloppy brown slush and looked in all the shop windows with lights and cotton wool snow.

When they got home, they put the shopping away as fast as they could and peeled the potatoes and browned the meat and rolled the pastry and put the pie in the oven and cleared a space.

"Now then," said Josie's mum, and she got the tissue paper out of its bag.

"What are you making?" asked Josie Smith.

"Watch and you'll see," said Josie's mum. "And find me an elastic band from the drawer."

Josie's mum spread out the tissue paper with the pink sheet on top of the blue sheet. Then she began to pleat it, under and over and under and over, until it was one thin strip. She twisted the long strip in the middle and folded it in half and said, "Watch." She tied the fold with the elastic band and put it in Josie Smith's hand. "Watch it open," she said, and she started to open the pleats and they opened and opened and opened and opened and a flower grew out of them.

"A flower!" shouted Josie Smith. "A flower as big as me!"

She jumped up and down and then she stopped and said, "Why am I having a flower?"

"Wait and see," said Josie's mum. "Now, get your wellingtons and wipe them clean and make them nice and shiny."

Josie's mum lent Josie Smith a pair of black tights that were hers. "They'll be too big for you," she said. "But you can tuck them right under your toes."

Josie Smith pulled on the tights and tucked them right under her toes. Then she put her wellingtons on.

Josie's mum got her old jumper out of a drawer. It had yellow and brown stripes and a little hole in the sleeve and a drawstring round the bottom. Josie Smith didn't like the old jumper but she liked the flower, so she didn't say anything. Then Josie's mum brought a black woolly hat and a needle and thread and the scrap of dark blue net and the eiderdown from Josie's doll's pram.

"What am I being?" asked Josie Smith.

"You'll see," said Josie's mum. "Now take off your kilt and your cardigan and close your eyes."

Josie Smith took off her kilt and cardigan and closed her eyes. She felt the old jumper go over her head and the eiderdown go round her tummy. Then she felt the jumper come down over the eiderdown and the string at the bottom being tied. Then she didn't feel anything.

"What are you doing now?" asked Josie Smith.

"Threading my needle," said Josie's mum. "Stand still and keep your eyes shut." Josie Smith stood still while her mum did some sewing behind her back. Then she pulled the hat down over Josie's head and said, "Come in the front room and see."

They went in the front room where there

was a big mirror for ladies to try on their dresses.

"Open your eyes," said Josie's mum.

Josie Smith opened her eyes and saw a fat brown and yellow striped body and a little black head and thin black legs, and when she turned round she had blue net wings.

"I'm a bee!" shouted Josie Smith. "A bee! A bumble bee!"

"That's why you need a flower," said Josie's mum. "And you'll need a sting, as well. We'll make you one after dinner."

Josie Smith ate two plates of pie, and every now and then she said, "Zzzzz."

After dinner they made a sting from cardboard, crayoned black, and stuck it on like a tail.

"Now put your coat on," said Josie's mum. "It's time for you to set off."

Josie Smith put her coat on and her itchy scarf and took her flower and went to call for Eileen.

Eileen's dad came and opened the door and he said, "You'd better come in for a minute. Our Eileen's crying."

Josie Smith went in. Eileen was standing in the middle of the room with her crinoline dress and her crook and her lamb and she was roaring. Her face was red and her cheeks were wet and she kept stamping her stockinged feet.

"She wants to go in her ballet shoes," said Eileen's mum. On the floor was a pair of black ballet shoes with bows on them for Eileen's costume, and next to that her red wellingtons.

"It's wet outside," said Eileen's mum. "And filthy too."

"Let's be having you," said Eileen's dad. "Time's getting on."

Josie Smith waited, holding her flower.

Eileen screamed and screamed.

When they set off, Eileen had her ballet shoes on and her dad had to carry her and her wellingtons all the way. Eileen smiled a little smile and looked down at Josie Smith.

They had to walk a long way. When they were walking along, Josie Smith held her flower up to show it to Eileen. Eileen looked down at it and said, "You have to wear wellingtons because you haven't got a dad to carry you."

Josie Smith looked at Eileen's feet dangling down in their brand new white socks and new black ballet shoes with bows on them and she wished she had a dad and some ballet shoes.

"When we get inside," said Eileen's dad, "stick to my hand or I'll lose you both."

They went up some big stone steps and stood in a queue with hundreds of people. Eileen's dad put Eileen down.

Eileen stared at Josie Smith and said, "You're supposed to have a costume on because it's a fancy dress party."

"I have got a costume on," said Josie Smith.

"You haven't," Eileen said, "You've just got your coat on and your wellingtons and a stupid black hat. That's not a costume."

"Give me your coats," said Eileen's dad.

They gave him their coats and Josie Smith the bee started buzzing.

"Zzzzz! Zzzzz!" she went, and she turned round and put her sting near Eileen's leg.

"Ow! It's a bee!" Eileen shouted. "It's a

bee and it's stinging me!" And they started giggling and chasing each other.

Then Eileen's dad took them into the biggest room that Josie Smith had ever seen. It was so high that you nearly had to go right over backwards to look at the Christmas decorations hanging across the ceiling, and so big that there were hundreds and hundreds of children with costumes on running about and sliding all over the shiny floor and there was still room for hundreds more. At the other end there was a stage with a giant Christmas tree with silver streamers on it and a man who was shouting things and clapping his hands.

Josie Smith and Eileen charged into the middle of the big shiny floor and started shouting and sliding with everybody else. There were balloons everywhere and they batted them and kicked them and caught them and burst them. They saw Wee Willie Winkie in pyjamas with a candle and it was Gary Grimes, and Josie Smith stung him and made him run away. Then they saw Batman and it was Rawley Baxter, and Josie

Smith stung him and he pretended to run away. Then they saw an Indian chief and it was Jimmy Earnshaw, and Josie Smith said "Zzzzz!" But she didn't sting him and he laughed and gave her a pink balloon.

Then the man on the stage clapped his hands and shouted and everybody went pushing and screaming into another big room where there were long tables with twists of crepe paper across them and paper plates with holly and a cracker near each one. And they all sat down on benches and ate muffins with turkey and stuffing and jelly and blancmange and biscuits with pink and white sugar patterns and slices of hard Christmas cake with silver balls on the icing that hurt your teeth, and Gary Grimes spilled pink blancmange all down the front of his pyjamas.

When they were so full they were bursting they all pulled their crackers and went pushing and screaming back into the big room. The Christmas tree was lit up with coloured lights and the man on the stage clapped his hands and they all had to sit on the floor.

A lady played the piano and they sang 'Rudolph the Red Nosed Reindeer' and 'White Christmas' and 'Jingle Bells' and 'When Santa Got Stuck up the Chimney', and the man on the stage kept looking the other way and then he waved to somebody and then he looked down at all the children and clapped his hands and said:

"Do we want Father Christmas to come?"

And the children all shouted, "Yes!"

And the man said, "Do we want him to come now?"

And the children all shouted, "Yes!"

"All right, then!" said the man on the stage, "I want you all to sing 'Jingle Bells' as loud as you can."

So they all sang 'Jingle Bells' and the man on the stage shouted, "Louder! Louder! He can't hear you!"

And they all roared 'Jingle Bells' and Josie Smith roared so loud that she made her throat and her ears hurt and then Father Christmas came.

He came on the stage with his red coat and hood and his big white beard, dragging a huge sack of presents behind him.

"Hooray!" roared all the children. "Hooray!" And they all got up and started pushing. Josie Smith got up but somebody stood on her toe and somebody else knocked her down again and trod on her flower and dirtied it. She stood up again carefully and rubbed the dirt off her flower with her striped sleeve. Then she waited quietly. She didn't want to try and push to the front because her flower would get ripped to pieces. She waited a long time. Sometimes she could just see the pointy top of Father Christmas's hood over the children's heads. Sometimes, when big children pushed in front of her, she couldn't see anything. There were children pushing back the other way now, tearing the wrapping paper off their presents from Father Christmas. The boys' presents were wrapped in blue tissue paper and the girls' in pink. Soon there was ripped tissue paper all over the floor and Josie Smith was still at the back of the queue. She started worrying. There

might not be enough presents for so many children. A boy in a cowboy outfit said, "It's not really Father Christmas, anyway. I bet it's just somebody's dad dressed up." A fat little girl who was holding his hand started crying.

"Shut up crying," the cowboy said.

The fat little girl was wearing a fairy frock with a wand and glasses. She didn't stop crying. "I want my present," she screamed. "There'll be no present left for me."

"Don't be stupid," the cowboy said. "He's got all our names written down, my dad said."

Josie Smith's chest was going bam bam bam! Did Father Christmas have her name written down? Who would have told it to him? Did Eileen's dad tell him she was coming as well as Eileen? And what if he'd forgotten? Eileen could tell him when she went up for her present, but Josie Smith couldn't see Eileen any more. She couldn't see the cowboy and the fairy any more, either. All the children around her were opening their pink and blue parcels. Nobody else was still waiting except her. Josie Smith held her flower carefully and pushed nearer to the stage. A big space opened out in front of her and she saw the man clapping his hands and shouting. But the big sack was gone and all the presents were gone and Father Christmas had gone, too.

Josie Smith felt a big lump coming in her throat to make her cry. She held her flower as tight as she could and squeezed her eyes shut so the tears couldn't get out because she didn't want to be a cry-baby.

Then somebody got hold of her hand and she opened her eyes again. The piano was playing again and all the children were walking round and round the edge of the room in twos. The lady who had got hold of Josie Smith's hand said, "Come on, love. Don't you want to join in?"

She took Josie Smith and made her walk next to a great big box with legs sticking out the bottom and no head. An arm came out the side of it and a sticky warm hand got hold of Josie Smith's hand. Josie Smith didn't want to walk round with the horrible box so she didn't hold hands back, she just left her hand where it was and thought about walking round in time to the music. She felt hot and tired and a bit frightened.

Once when they were going round she saw Eileen a long way away, right at the other end of the room. She was holding hands with two other Bo Peeps with frocks and lambs like hers. Round and round they went. Round and round and round. The grown-ups were sitting on chairs round the edge and they were laughing and pointing and talking. Josie Smith couldn't see Eileen's dad. The man on the stage kept shouting things and they still kept going round and round. Round and round and round.

"Third prize!" he shouted. The music stopped and they all stood still for a minute and the grown-ups clapped. Then the music started and they set off again. Round and round. Round and round and round. Josie Smith's feet felt too hot in her wellingtons and every time she looked down at them she saw piles of pink and blue tissue paper that made the lump come back in her throat to make her cry because she hadn't got a present from Father Christmas. She squeezed her eyes shut again.

"Second prize!" shouted the man on the stage and the music stopped and they all stood still while the grown-ups clapped. The lady who had made Josie Smith walk with the horrible box came and took it away while they were clapping. Josie Smith was glad when the warm sticky hand let go of hers. She wiped it a bit on her jumper. Then the music started and they set off again. But now Josie Smith was by herself. She walked a few steps and then stopped and wondered what to do. Nobody else was walking by

themselves and, anyway, when she'd waited to wipe her hand before setting off again she'd lost her place.

Two girls in long paper frocks and tinsel crowns came past and Josie Smith started going round again near them. But one of the girls nipped her and said, "You have to walk round in twos." So she stopped again.

It wasn't true, anyway, because she'd seen Eileen walking with two other girls. But perhaps you had to be dressed the same. Josie Smith stood still and watched but she couldn't see another bee going round. Then, right across the other side of the room she saw Gary Grimes and he was going round by himself. She set off to go and walk with him but then she got frightened and stopped.

The other side was miles away across the big shiny floor with tissue paper and streamers and biscuits and a big puddle of something that looked like lemonade. Josie Smith stood there where everybody could stare at her and she shut her eyes so they wouldn't see her and whispered, "I want to go home."

But she couldn't go home because there was nobody to take her. She couldn't see Eileen's dad any more, or even Eileen, and she couldn't go by herself because she couldn't remember the way.

"First prize!" shouted the man on the stage, and the music stopped. Josie Smith tried and tried to remember the road they had come down but all she could remember was Eileen's ballet shoes and then the big stone steps.

"Bumble bee!" shouted the man on the stage, and everybody clapped.

Josie Smith started crying. She didn't

know where she was, but what if her mum didn't know where she was either?

"Bumble bee!" shouted the man on the stage, and this time Josie Smith heard him and she really started to roar. Now they were going to shout at her for going round by herself when it wasn't her fault!

Josie Smith roared and roared and the lady came again and got hold of her hand. Josie Smith was crying so hard that she couldn't see where she was going or hear what everybody was saying. Somebody lifted her up, and when she opened her eyes she was on the stage and everybody was laughing and clapping. Josie Smith held her flower tight.

The man on the stage bent down to her and said, "What's the matter with you?"

"I want to go home," said Josie Smith. "And I didn't get a present from Father Christmas."

"You didn't?" the man said, "And why not?"

"I don't know," said Josie Smith.

"Well, that won't do," said the man on the stage. "Now, you catch hold of your

prize." And he gave Josie Smith a big doll in a flowered box with cellophane on the front. Then he went away and Josie Smith waited, holding the doll in the box and her flower.

When he came back, he gave Josie Smith a present in pink tissue paper and said, "You were lucky there. He was just getting into his sleigh out the back when I caught him."

Josie Smith held the doll in the box and the present in pink tissue paper and her flower and she stopped crying.

Then she jumped down from the stage and shouted, "Mum!"

And there was Josie's mum coming to get her with her raincoat on and Josie's coat in one hand and an umbrella in the other.

"It's pouring down," said Josie's mum. "So I thought I'd slip down with Eileen's mum and bring you a couple of umbrellas."

Then she said, "Have you had a good time?"

"Yes," said Josie Smith. "And I got a prize and a present from Father Christmas."

"Let me put your scarf on," said Josie's

mum. "What's the matter with your face? Have you been crying?"

"A bit," said Josie Smith.

"What for?" said Josie's mum.

"I can't remember," said Josie Smith. She fastened her coat and got hold of her flower and the doll in the box and her present and they went to look for Eileen.

"I'm putting my wellies on," Eileen said. "And then I can walk with you. Your costume won first prize. If you let me wear it when we get home, you can wear mine."

And all the way home they stamped their wellingtons in the puddles, holding hands and singing 'Jingle Bells' loud enough to make Father Christmas come. Because even if Eileen was horrible sometimes, she was still Josie Smith's best friend.

Josie Smith and Percy

"I'll tell you a secret, if you want," said Eileen.

"What is it?" asked Josie Smith.

It was hot in the classroom. The lights were on and everything smelled of fish. Josie Smith and Eileen were sitting together at their table crayoning Christmas cards to take home for their mums. Gary Grimes was scribbling on his and Rawley Baxter had done a horrible drawing of Batman whizzing through the sky with a crooked Christmas star in the top corner.

"Behold!" shouted Rawley Baxter. "I bring you tidings of great joy! Wheeeeee!"

"Shut up, Rawley Baxter," Eileen said. "And anyway, you're supposed to say 'We have followed a bright star.' I'm the one who says 'Tidings of great joy'."

"I don't care," Rawley Baxter said. And he started scribbling black sky round his crooked star.

"It's all black, your picture," Eileen said. "It doesn't look like a Christmas card at all."

"Mind your own business," Rawley Baxter said.

"Give us the black," Gary Grimes said, and he started scribbling a black sky as well.

"Copy cat," said Eileen, and then she said to Josie Smith, "Will you draw me a robin like yours?"

"I will, if you want," said Josie Smith. "But you have to tell me the secret."

So Josie Smith drew a robin on a snowy branch on Eileen's card and Eileen watched. Then she put her hand near her mouth and whispered in Josie Smith's ear, "There is no Father Christmas. It's just your dad dressed up."

"That's stupid," Josie Smith said. "If there was no Father Christmas we wouldn't get any presents." Then she turned the other way and dug Rawley Baxter in the arm and said, "Do you want me to draw a robin for

you, as well? Then you'll have Batman and
Robin!"

Gary Grimes laughed but Rawley Baxter
took no notice. He flew his plastic Batman
over the one on his Christmas card and made
them talk to each other.

"Quiet, now!" Miss Valentine said. "Finish
your cards as quickly as you can because
we've got to put our decorations up today."

They were quiet for a bit, crayoning hard,
and they could hear somebody practising
in the hall and the piano playing. Josie
Smith crayoned a bunch of holly and

Eileen watched her. Then she crayoned Father Christmas coming out the top of a chimney with his sack and waving, and Eileen said, "There is no Father Christmas and I know how you get your presents. They're all hidden on the top of the wardrobe and then on Christmas Eve your dad dresses up and puts them out for you."

"You're a liar!" Josie Smith said, and her chest was going bam bam bam because she was upset. "Father Christmas comes to my house and I leave him a mince pie on the fender and he eats it, so there!"

"He does not," Eileen said. "And anyway, my presents are on top of the wardrobe and I've seen them and I know what's in some of them."

Josie Smith crayoned Father Christmas's red coat and didn't say anything. Eileen spoilt her robin with a brown crayon.

"You shouldn't scribble," Josie Smith said. "You've spoilt it now." Then she wrote above Father Christmas's head MERY CHRISTMAS FROM UP IN THE SKY. And on the inside, LOVE FROM JOSIE.

"You've spelt Merry Christmas wrong," said Eileen.

"You can't spell, anyway," said Josie Smith.

"I can spell Merry Christmas," Eileen said, "because Miss Valentine wrote it on the wall for us to copy."

On the wall was a big sheet of pale green paper with some holly drawn in the corner with magic markers. Miss Valentine had written Merry Christmas and a Happy New Year to help them.

Josie Smith tried to fit another R in Mery but it wouldn't go.

Miss Valentine gave out packets of gummed paper strips to make paper chains. Then she started cutting crepe paper fringes to stick over the light shades. When she climbed up the ladder and stuck them on, the classroom looked Christmassy and coloured like a magic cave.

Josie Smith made paper chains as fast as she could and thought about Christmas and then about Father Christmas and then about what Eileen had said. How could Father Christmas really be your dad? Josie Smith

hadn't got a dad but her presents came just the same, so Eileen was stupid.

"Come on, now," Miss Valentine said up her ladder, "let's get these chains up."

Josie Smith's chain was long. Eileen's was short. Rawley Baxter hadn't even started his and Gary Grimes's chain was all soggy and ripped and dirty because he'd licked all the glue off and it was only stuck together with spit. They took them to Miss Valentine and all the other tables took theirs and Miss Valentine hung them up.

"Thank goodness that's done," she said,

as she was climbing down the ladder. Then Gary Grimes's soggy chain fell to pieces and all the other chains came down with it and covered Miss Valentine and the ladder and all the tables. Miss Valentine looked as if she were going to cry. Then she started laughing and they all laughed and the bell went for home time.

"Get your coats on," Miss Valentine said. "I'll put these up when you've gone. And don't forget your Christmas cards."

They all said Goo-daf-ter-noon-Miss-Valen-tine and then they set off home.

Josie Smith didn't want to walk home with Eileen. She ran off fast in her wellingtons in the wet and the fog and followed Rawley Baxter who was running with his coat held out and shouting Batman!

When she turned the corner and got to her own front door she didn't go in. She went on running right to the bottom of the street until she got to her gran's. She had to go to her gran's because her mum had gone to a lady's house to measure her for a wedding dress.

"Sit you down," said Josie's gran. "Only

take those wellingtons off first. They look wet to me."

"They are wet," said Josie Smith.

"You could do with a pair of slippers to keep here," said Josie's gran. "Put this pair of mine on. You'll not be able to walk in them but they'll keep your feet warm."

Josie Smith put her gran's slippers on and she did walk in them, doing great big loopy steps and laughing at her tiny legs and giant feet.

"Gran?" she said, when she sat down to her tea, "I've asked Father Christmas to bring me some slippers with fur inside and pompoms on like Eileen's, and if he does I can bring my old ones here to leave."

"That's a good idea," said Josie's gran. "Do you want another cup of tea?"

"I haven't finished this one," said Josie Smith, "because it's hot. Gran?"

"What, love?"

"Eileen said . . ."

"What did Eileen say?" asked Josie's gran.

"Eileen said there's no Father Christmas, it's just everybody's dad who dresses up as him, but it's not, is it, Gran?"

"I wouldn't have thought so," said Josie's gran. "Not everybody has a dad, now do they? How about one of these buns?"

"Yes please. But, Gran? Eileen's stupid because when we went to the fancy dress party Father Christmas was there and we saw him and he gave us a present."

"Well," said Josie's gran, "there you are then. Now don't talk with your mouth full." And she gave Josie Smith two buns in a bag to take home and looked out through the lace curtains and said, "Your mum's back, I can see the light. Off you go and I'll be watching."

"But Gran," said Josie Smith, pulling her socks up and getting into her wellingtons, "Eileen says her presents are on top of the wardrobe. She says she's seen them and she says she knows what's in some of them."

"Well, they're not real Christmas presents then, are they?" said Josie's gran. "They'll just be a few things her mum's bought her. You know how she's always buying her things."

"She's spoilt, Eileen," Josie Smith said. "My mum said."

"Well, don't you bother," said Josie's gran. "You write a nice letter to Father Christmas and then there can be no mistake. Go on, now. I'm watching."

And Josie Smith ran home.

The next day was Saturday. Josie Smith and Josie's mum wrapped up well and went out in the foggy cold to do the shopping.

They queued in the butcher's that was full to bursting and had mistletoe and a red ribbon hanging from the ceiling. They waited and waited and Josie Smith drew patterns in the sawdust with her wellington and her mum bought stewing steak and fat, pale sausages and ordered a turkey "not too big".

They queued in Kefford's, the greengrocer's that was full of big ladies talking, and Mr Kefford gave Josie Smith a tangerine and Josie Smith sniffed its skin that smelled of Christmas day. They bought potatoes, onions, cabbage and carrots and ordered Brussels sprouts and dates in a box with a frill round and camels on the lid. Then they chose a Christmas tree from the pile in the back and Mr Kefford promised to bring it when he'd shut his shop.

When they came out, Josie Smith said, "Are we going to pay the papers?"

"Oh, good heavens," said Josie's mum, "I should have remembered before we bought all these heavy things."

Josie Smith put her tangerine in her pocket and carried the bag of potatoes. When they got to Mr Bowker's newsagent's, Josie Smith stopped and said, "Can I look in the window at the toys?"

"All right," said Josie's mum. "But see that you stay right there."

"I will," said Josie Smith, and she pressed her nose to the window to look. There were dots of cotton wool snow on the window and Christmas lights around it that winked on and off. At the bottom there was an electric train going round and round a track and up a little hill and through a tunnel at the back. It stayed in the tunnel for a long time and then it came round again. Josie Smith liked the train. Its engine was dark green with black stripes. Up one side of the window there were shiny new books, picture books, story books and annuals. All up the other side there were shelves with flat boxes with chemistry sets and post office sets and dolls' hairdressing sets.

Josie Smith looked at them all and then she looked up at the back of the window where all the dolls were lined up. There were baby dolls with dummies and Barbie dolls with clothes and bride dolls and boy dolls and long-haired dolls with combs. But right in the middle of all these dolls Josie Smith saw something else. Somebody else was looking out at Josie Smith looking in, with brown eyes just like hers. Josie Smith held her breath and pressed her nose hard against the window and rubbed at the steam with her glove.

It was a panda. Not like an ordinary toy panda but just like a real panda sitting up with his fat paws sticking out and his fat tummy sticking out and a big woolly head bigger than Josie Smith's own. Josie Smith stared in at the panda and the panda stared out at Josie Smith with sad black patches round his bright brown eyes.

"Percy," whispered Josie Smith, because he looked just like a panda who would be called Percy.

Percy waited, looking at her.

"Percy," whispered Josie Smith. "I'm going to ask my mum if I can have you. And if you cost a lot of money I won't ask for anything else, not even fur slippers with pompoms on or marbles or a book. I won't even put my stocking out for nuts and tangerines and chocolates. And anyway, Mr Kefford gave me a tangerine and I can save that."

Percy waited, listening.

"I'll have to ask my mum," Josie Smith

explained to him, "if she thinks Father Christmas will bring you. I'm going in now or else somebody might buy you before I can ask her."

Josie Smith ran in at the newsagent's door, ringing the bell.

"Mum! Mum! There's a panda called Percy in the window and I want him for Christmas! Mum, can I? And I won't ask for anything else, not even a tangerine! Can I?"

"Wait a minute," said Josie's mum, "we're just doing the bill."

Josie Smith waited, holding her bag of

potatoes. She felt out of breath because she was excited and frightened that somebody would come in and buy Percy before she could tell her mum. She tried to see into the window from inside the shop but she couldn't.

"Mum . . . !" she whispered, but not loud enough for her mum to hear because she didn't want her to get mad. When the bill was paid, Mr Bowker the newsagent looked over the counter at Josie Smith and said, "I heard about you winning first prize at the fancy dress party."

"I did," said Josie Smith. "And Father Christmas came and gave us all a present as well."

She waited to see if Mr Bowker would say there was no Father Christmas but he didn't. And Mr Bowker knew, because a lot of Father Christmas's presents came from his shop.

"We'd better get to Mrs Chadwick's," said Josie's mum, "or there won't be a loaf or a teacake left."

"But Mum!" shouted Josie Smith. "I want you to look at Percy!"

"Percy?" said Josie's mum. "Who's Percy?"

"He's a panda," said Josie Smith, looking at her mum as hard as she could to make her listen. "He's in the window."

"A panda?" said Josie's mum. "What panda?"

But Mr Bowker laughed and said, "I'll get him out for you."

"We ought to be going," said Josie's mum, but Josie Smith put her bag down and held on to her hand as tight as she could and they didn't go.

Mr Bowker lifted Percy out and sat him on the counter. Josie Smith held her breath and Percy looked at her with his big brown eyes and waited.

"Isn't he lovely," said Josie's mum, and she stroked his big woolly head.

"Can I touch him?" whispered Josie Smith.

"If your hands are clean," said Josie's mum.

Josie Smith pulled her gloves off and stuffed them in her pocket. Her mum lifted her up a bit so she could reach and she touched Percy's fur just a tiny bit. Then she put her face near his bigger face and sniffed. He smelled of brand new fur and Christmas. Josie's mum put her down.

"Can I have him?" asked Josie Smith. "Can I ask Father Christmas for him? I won't ask for anything else if I can have him. Can I, Mum?"

"Well," said Josie's mum. "We'll have to see."

"But if we have to see," said Josie Smith, "somebody might buy him and take him away and he wants to come with me!"

"I'll see they don't take him away," Mr Bowker said. "You write to Father Christmas about it. Percy will wait."

And he put Percy back in the window.

That night, when Josie Smith went to bed she told her angel on the chest of drawers about Percy. "And the Christmas tree's come and tomorrow you can go on it, right at the top."

So the next day Josie Smith and Josie's mum decorated the Christmas tree and put the angel right at the top. And when she'd had a bath ready for school next day, Josie Smith sat under the tree in her pyjamas to write to Father Christmas.

The carpet was all prickly with pine needles under the tree but Josie Smith liked the smell of them so she stayed there anyway.

Dear Father Christmas, wrote Josie Smith. How are you? I am very well. When we were at the fancy dress party I couldn't come on the stage because I was at the back and I had to hold my flower. Thank you for my present. For Christmas I would like Percy

Panda. You don't need to bring some fur slippers with pompoms and marbles and a book and a stocking with tangerines. I can just have Percy. He is at Mr Bowker's shop. I hope you are well. I hope you like your mince pie. Love from Josie.

"Mum?" said Josie Smith when she'd finished, "Can I post my letter?"

"We'll see," said Josie's mum. "You know you can't go to the letter box by yourself. It's on the main road."

On Monday afternoon after school, Josie Smith went to her gran's and told her about the letter.

"Will you take me, Gran? Please? I can't go by myself because it's on the main road."

"All right," said Josie's gran. "But you'll want something nice and warm on your head in this weather."

"I'll put my hood up," said Josie Smith.

But her gran tied a great big itchy woolly headscarf round her head and made a big knot under her chin and then made her put her hood up as well. Then she wrapped herself up and took her umbrella and they went to post the letter.

"Does it need a stamp on it?" asked Josie Smith.

"Not for Father Christmas," said Josie's gran.

Josie Smith put the letter in the slot very carefully and then said, "Can we go just a bit further up the road and look in Mr Bowker's window?"

"All right," said Josie's gran. "Just for a few minutes."

When they got there, Percy was sitting in his place, waiting. Josie Smith pressed her nose to the cold window and whispered, "I've asked Father Christmas for you." And she looked hard at Percy and Percy looked hard at her.

"Can you see any marbles . . . ?" said Josie's gran.

Then they went home.

On Tuesday at school, when they were having a dress rehearsal for the Nativity play, Eileen put her tinsel halo on and said, "I'm having some fur gloves for Christmas as well as my nurse's uniform and a ballet dress."

"Well!" said Josie Smith, "I'm having fur

slippers!" But then she remembered Percy and said, "I was going to, but now I don't want them any more." Josie Smith felt her prickly halo and she was pleased because she was being an angel and because she was only having Percy for Christmas. She wanted to go and see him after school, if somebody would take her.

"Gran!" she shouted, running in at her gran's front door after school.

"Are you here again?" said Josie's gran. "Is your mum out?"

"No," said Josie Smith. "But she said I could come and ask you to take me up the road with my spending money to buy her a present for Christmas. Will you, Gran?"

"Well," said Josie's gran, "you'd better have something on your head."

So they wrapped themselves up in itchy headscarves and set off.

"What are you going to buy her?" asked Josie's gran.

"Some perfume or else some nail varnish," said Josie Smith.

"But she doesn't wear nail varnish," said Josie's gran.

"She might wear it," said Josie Smith, "if she had some. I'd wear nail varnish if I was a grown-up."

"You buy her a nice little bottle of scent."

So they bought a nice little bottle of scent and Josie Smith gave all her saved up spending money to the chemist and her gran gave him a bit as well to help. The chemist wrapped the box of perfume up in Christmas paper and put a bit of red ribbon round it while Josie Smith stamped her wellingtons on the wet floor and looked at the rows of nail varnish bottles with pointy handles on the counter.

When they got outside, Josie Smith said, "Gran? Can we go just a bit further up the road and look in Mr Bowker's window?"

"All right," said Josie's gran. "Just for a minute."

When they got there, Percy was sitting in his place, waiting.

Josie Smith pressed her nose to the cold window and whispered, "I've bought a present for my mum," and she looked in at Percy and Percy looked out at her.

"They've some lovely new books, haven't they?" said Josie's gran.

Then they went home.

Wednesday was the last day at school and in the afternoon they had drawing and Josie Smith crayoned a specially nice picture with holly and snow and an angel. It was to give to her gran for a Christmas present. After playtime they had a party in their classroom and everybody put paper hats on, even Miss Valentine. They ate sandwiches and jelly and a tube of toffees each and a bun with white icing and silver balls on it.

When all the food was gone and all the paper hats were ripped except Eileen's and Gary Grimes had been sick, they all got their coats on to go home.

"Now, you must all be back here by six o'clock," Miss Valentine said, "and ready in your costumes at a quarter past."

It was funny going up to school at night with her mum. Josie Smith liked it, but she wished she'd had time to go with her gran to see Percy and tell him about it. When they were on the stage and Eileen lifted her arms up to say "Behold I bring you tidings of great joy", Josie Smith stood very still with her hands joined and tried to look like her angel at home on the Christmas tree.

And when Rawley Baxter lifted up one hand to point and said, "Behold I bring you tidings of great joy", instead of "We have followed a bright star", nobody noticed and all the mums and dads clapped and they sang two carols.

Josie Smith and Eileen went home in their coats with their long frocks and halos on because their mums said they could.

The next day it was Christmas Eve.

Josie Smith and Josie's mum went out in the foggy wet cold to do their Christmas shopping. They went to the butcher's and queued up for their turkey and said Merry Christmas. They went to the greengrocer's to buy sprouts and tangerines and dates and nuts and said Merry Christmas. They went to Mr Bowker's to buy some wrapping paper for Josie's mum's present to Josie's gran, and Josie Smith stayed outside to look at Percy and say Merry Christmas.

But Percy had gone.

The train was there, going round and through the tunnel and out again. The books were there and the chemistry sets and the post office sets and the dolls' hairdressing sets. But at the back, in the middle of all the dolls, was a dart board.

Josie Smith's chest was going bam bam bam when her mum came out of Mr Bowker's and they set off down the road.

They went in Mrs Chadwick's and bought some flour and sugar and icing sugar and a jar of mincemeat, and Josie's mum said Merry Christmas, but Josie Smith didn't say anything because she had a lump in

her throat.

In the afternoon, Eileen came round. Josie's mum was busy in the kitchen making mince pies and stuffing for the turkey so they played in the front room where the Christmas tree was.

"I've opened one of my presents," Eileen said. "It's an annual, and I've done one of the dot-to-dot pictures already and it's a giraffe. My other presents are on the wardrobe."

Josie Smith didn't say anything.

At bedtime, Josie's mum said, "You're

very quiet. What's to do with you?"

Josie Smith tried to swallow the lump in her throat and said, "Has Father Christmas taken Percy from Mr Bowker's window so he can bring him here?"

Josie's mum laughed and said, "You'll have to wait and see, won't you? Here's your mince pie to put out, and your stocking."

Josie Smith put the mince pie on the fender but she folded the stocking up and put it out of the way behind the Christmas tree so Father Christmas would remember that he didn't have to fill it. She tied her mum's present to one of the branches and propped the picture for her gran on another, where she'd see it when she arrived for her Christmas dinner. Then she remembered her tangerine that Mr Kefford had given her and she ran and got it from her coat pocket and put it near the tree to have next day instead of her stocking. Then she went to bed.

Josie Smith lay in the dark for a long time with her eyes open, thinking. Then she got out of bed very quietly and climbed on a chair. She reached up and felt on top of her

wardrobe. There was no Percy, only some
dust and fluff. She got down and went to the
top of the stairs to listen. She heard the front
door open and her gran coming in and then
a lot of talking. She could smell some more
mince pies baking. She waited a bit till they
really got talking downstairs and then she
crept across to her mum's bedroom. There
was a yellow cardigan lying on a chair near
the bed and a pair of shoes on the rug. Josie
Smith looked at the wardrobe. It was very

high. She climbed on the chair with the cardigan but she couldn't reach. Then she climbed sideways on to the dressing table and her chest was going bam bam bam because she knew she shouldn't. She shut her eyes tight so that nobody would see her and reached up to feel on top of the wardrobe. There was no Percy, only some dust and fluff. Josie Smith climbed down and went back to bed and curled up to try and warm her feet. If there were no presents on the wardrobe that meant that Father Christmas must be coming. But was he bringing Percy? Or had somebody been in the shop and bought him?

Josie Smith felt lonely. She missed having her angel to talk to, and even Ginger the cat hadn't come up to sleep near her because he liked sleeping on the rug in front of the fire in winter. Josie Smith jumped out of bed again and sat down on the windowsill with the curtain round her, looking out.

She would wait up for Father Christmas and see him and talk to him, that was best. She sat still for a long time.

She listened for sleigh bells but she only heard some cars going past. She stared at the rows and rows of black chimneys but nobody popped out waving and pulling a sack. She looked for the light from Rudolph's red nose but there was only the sad yellowy light from the same old lamp post at the corner. Josie Smith fell asleep.

When she woke up she was freezing and her mum was coming upstairs to bed. She jumped in under the covers and shut her eyes. She heard her mum stop and look in to see if she was covered up and then go away.

Josie Smith waited and listened in the dark. She didn't know how long she'd been asleep. Perhaps Father Christmas had been already. Josie Smith got up and crept downstairs in her striped pyjamas. The front room was very quiet and smelled of the Christmas tree. The angel and the tinsel and the coloured balls sparkled in the bit of light from the fire that was going out. Ginger was asleep on the rug and the mince pie was still on the fender.

Josie Smith sat down on the settee with

her feet on the rug near Ginger.

"I'm waiting," she whispered. "I'm waiting and I'll tell him . . ."

But she was so tired that she couldn't remember what she wanted to tell him. She laid her head down on the arm of the settee and tried hard to keep her eyes open and watch the chimney. She had to stay awake a bit longer because he couldn't come before the fire went out. After a while, she couldn't remember any more whether she was awake or not. And after that she was fast asleep.

Then it was Christmas morning and some new smells tickled her nose and woke her up. She opened her sleepy eyes a little bit and saw a new fire just getting going with damp wood and newspaper spitting and smoking. That's what was tickling her nose. But something else was tickling her nose too. Somebody else was cuddled up to her face and it wasn't Ginger. Josie Smith opened her eyes wider and sniffed a smell of brand new fur and Christmas.

"Percy!"

And it was Percy! He was snuggled right up to her and his head was bigger than her head and both of them were covered by the eiderdown from Josie's bed.

Josie Smith sat up in the eiderdown, holding Percy tight, and shouted, "Mum!"

"Merry Christmas," said Josie's mum, and she came in with two mugs of cocoa. "And now you can tell me just what you've been doing down here all night."

"I was waiting for Father Christmas," said Josie Smith.

"Well, you missed him," said Josie's mum. "I came down early to put the turkey in the oven and what did I find?"

"Me!" shouted Josie Smith.

"You and Percy," said Josie's mum. "And Ginger as well but he's up having his breakfast now. You were all asleep in a pile with the eiderdown over you."

"I didn't bring my eiderdown in here," said Josie Smith.

"Well, somebody did," said Josie's mum. "And somebody brought Percy and somebody ate the mince pie you left on the fender."

Josie Smith looked.

"He's left some crumbs," she said.

"Well, I should think he was in a hurry," said Josie's mum. "Have you seen the other things he's left? Look."

Josie Smith looked. Under the tree there were two parcels, one that looked hard and square and one that looked soft and squashy.

"A book and fur slippers!" shouted Josie Smith.

"And a stocking," said Josie's mum. Father Christmas had found the stocking that Josie Smith had hidden and he'd filled it up.

Josie's mum brought the parcels and Percy sat on Josie's knee and they opened everything together. There were furry slippers with blue pompoms on the front and a shiny new book with pictures in it. And in the stocking there was a packet of new marbles and toffees and nuts and chocolate money and a tangerine in the toe.

Josie Smith and Josie's mum ate a chocolate coin with their cocoa because on Christmas day you can do everything you want. You can even eat chocolate for

breakfast. Ginger had finished his breakfast and he came back and stared at them. The fire got going and burned bright and warm and the angel glittered on the Christmas tree.

Josie Smith put on her new slippers with blue pompoms on and her tinsel halo from the Nativity play and snuggled up in a ball with her mum and Percy and Ginger and her eiderdown.

And when she was as warm as toast and happy enough to burst she said, "Mum? You know what? Eileen's daft and she says things back to front. It isn't everybody's dad who's Father Christmas. It's Father Christmas who's everybody's dad!"

Merry Christmas, Josie Smith.

Merry Christmas, Percy.